Praise for Nan McCarthy's
CHAT

"Draws you in from page to page. . . . Sequels are on the way, and I can hardly wait."
—L. R. Shannon, *The New York Times*

"By clever combinations of e-mail, live chat, emoticons, and computer shortcuts, she gives the headstrong-girl-meets-self-sufficient-boy story a refreshing twist."
—*Publishers Weekly*

"Could it be a high-tech version of *The Bridges of Madison County?* Bev and Max's letters are witty, hilarious, challenging, thoughtful, teasing, and full of tension. This isn't about those sleazy chat rooms. . . . CHAT is a hip look at the Internet cyber-culture and how it has changed the dynamic of present-day relationships."
—Tina Velgos, *The Review Zone*

Also by Nan McCarthy

CHAT
CRASH

Available from POCKET BOOKS

CONNECT

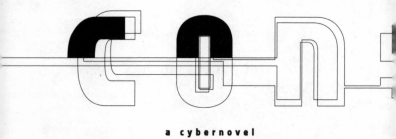

a cybernovel

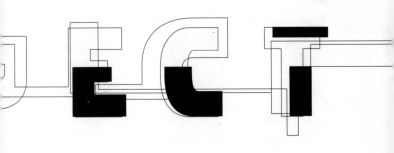

N A N M C C A R T H Y

POCKET BOOKS
New York London Toronto Sydney Tokyo Singapore

This book is a work of fiction. Names, characters, places, and incidents are products of the author's imagination or are used fictitiously. Any resemblance to actual events or locales or persons living or dead is entirely coincidental.

POCKET BOOKS, a division of Simon & Schuster Inc.
1230 Avenue of the Americas, New York, NY 10020

Copyright © 1996 by Nancy J. McCarthy

ISBN: 0-671-02340-3

First Pocket Books trade paperback printing October 1998

10 9 8 7 6 5 4 3 2 1

POCKET and colophon are registered trademarks of
Simon & Schuster Inc.

Cover design by Blacksheep

Cover photo by Tony Stone Images

Interior design by David J. High

Printed in the U.S.A.

FOR BEN

acknowledgments

When I wrote and self-published the first book in this series, CHAT, I was overwhelmed by the encouragement offered by my colleagues. Many people went out of their way to show their support, which helped me as I wrote and published CONNECT: Craig Kevghas, Rick Wallace, Joel Sironen, David Ambler, Linnea Dayton, Anita Dennis, Steve Collins, Scott Culley, Daniel Hammond, and Ted Nace.

Like most writers, my days are solitary. E-mail helps me connect with people, and I would like to thank my many cyber correspondents for their humorous, insightful, and inspirational messages: my friends from CompuServe's Desktop Publishing Forum, the Literary Forum Group, Studio B's Computer Book Publishing List, and especially Marsha Skrypuch, Mitch McCullough, Roger Everett, David Rogelberg, and Greg Compton. I would also like to thank my Web site designer, Eric Lewallen, for making all of my Web dreams come true, the late JB Whitwell, who e-mailed me the blonde joke that appears in Session One, and every one of the people who bought the first-edition copies of CHAT.

I could not lead such a fulfilling professional life without the balance and support provided by my family, and so I would like to thank my mother, my sister, my father-in-law and his new bride, and especially my husband Pat, for his faith in me, and my two sons Ben and Cole, for giving my life meaning.

—*Nan McCarthy, December 1996*

"To rage, to lust, to write to, to commend,
All is the purlieu of the god of love."
— *John Donne, "Love's Deity"*

preface

If you haven't had the experience of logging on to
the Internet or to a commercial online service, or
even if you don't yet own a computer, you can still
ease yourself into the new terminology of electronic
correspondence by glancing through the brief glossary of abbreviations, acronyms, and emoticons at the
back of this book. These shorthand words and sym-
bols help people who are communicating via e-mail
to inject emotion, tone, and even action into a medi-
um that would otherwise be devoid of the valuable
signals we often pick up when listening to a person's
voice on the telephone or observing facial expres-
sions and body language when talking in person.

So feel free to familiarize yourself with these online
terms by looking at the glossary before you start
reading CONNECT. Or, you can just dive right in,
and refer to the glossary after you've joined Bev and
Max on their wild ride through cyberspace.

— *Nan McCarthy*

CONNECT

member profile

Member Name: Beverly J.
ID: BevJ@frederic_gerard.com
Location: Midwest
Birth date: October 11
Sex: Female
Marital Status: Married
Computers: Mac Quadra and a PowerBook
Interests: Reading, playing the piano, studying
typography
Occupation: Editor
Quote: *Great works are performed not by strength but
by perseverance.*
　　　　　　　　　　　　　　　—Samuel Johnson

member profile

Member Name: Maximilian M.
ID: Maximilian@miller&morris.com
Location: Northern Hemisphere
Birth date: Taurus
Sex: male
Marital Status: single
Computers: who cares
Interests: bonsai gardening, writing poetry, mixing
the perfect martini
Occupation: copywriter
Quote: *For myself I live, live intensely and am fed by
life, and my value, whatever it be, is in my
own kind of expression of that.*
　　　　　　　　　　　　　　　—Henry James

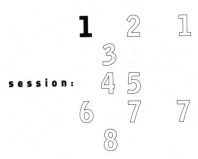

session: 1

> Private Mail
> Date: Monday, January 1, 1996 12:53 a.m.
> From: Maximilian@miller&morris.com
> Subj: Please
> To: BevJ@frederic_gerard.com

Beverly,

Why won't you answer my messages? I've been writing to you since the end of October—since the night
we last "spoke" online. Would you please send me
one response? I don't care if you tell me to go to
hell—I just want to hear from you and know that you
still exist and that what happened between us wasn't
a dream.

Besides, I still haven't figured out which Macintosh
to buy and I need your advice. <g>

Max

> Private Mail
> Date: Monday, January 8, 1996 11:41 p.m.
> From: Maximilian@miller&morris.com
> Subj: No Regrets
> To: BevJ@frederic_gerard.com

Bev,

Another week has gone by with no response from
you. I don't know why I thought I would hear from
you this time. You haven't answered any of my other
e-mails, so why would you answer the last one, or the
one before that, or this one, or the one after this
one?

I've thought about apologizing to you, but to tell you
the truth, I'm not sorry for anything that's happened
between you and me. I'm only sorry that you won't
talk to me anymore.

Max

> Private Mail
> Date: Monday, January 15, 1996 9:09 p.m.
> From: Maximilian@miller&morris.com
> Subj: Tiny Little Pieces
> To: BevJ@frederic_gerard.com

Hi Bev,

It's me, your old friend Max, sending you my weekly
monologue. I know you're receiving these messages—
or at least *someone* is receiving them—because
they're not bouncing back to me as undeliverable. So
either you are there and you're ignoring me, or you've
left your job and your office mates are retrieving
your mail and having themselves a knee-slapping
good time reading all of my pitiful pleadings to you.
Or maybe your husband is retrieving these messages
from your home computer because he found out
about us and he's already chopped you up into tiny
little pieces and put you in Ziploc baggies in the
deep freeze in the basement and is now trying to figure out how to track me down so he can do the same
to me. If so, hi Gary! How ya doin'? Wasn't Bev a
real piece of work?

Maximilian

> Private Mail
> Date: Monday, January 22, 1996 10:33 p.m.
> From: Maximilian@miller&morris.com
> Subj: <no subject>
> To: BevJ@frederic_gerard.com

Bev,

I know you're mad because I didn't tell you as soon
as I realized it that I was the stranger you had the
one-night stand with at Macworld. I let you continue
confiding in me about your feelings for that
"stranger" even after I figured out you were the
woman I had been with and had fallen in love with
that night. You think I made a fool of you, but I'm
the one who's a fool. I thought that by not telling
you who I really was, I could at least keep our
friendship going, even if I couldn't have you as my
lover. But the more we talked through e-mail, the
more deeply I fell in love with you. When you told
me you were wondering about the man you had the
affair with, what he was doing, if he was thinking
about you, I could barely contain myself. I hated the
way I was deceiving you, and I began to hate myself.
I went on a three-day martini binge and nearly got
fired from my job. I finally realized I had to tell you
who I was, even if that meant losing you. I knew
once you found out, you would be upset, just like you
are now. But there's a part of me that hopes I can
still get through to you, that something I'll say will
crack the surface and you'll open up to me once
again.

I miss you so.

Max

> Private Mail
> Date: Sunday, January 28, 1996 9:09 p.m.
> From: Maximilian@miller&morris.com
> Subj: thoughts of you
> To: BevJ@frederic_gerard.com

Bev,

I really didn't do much of anything today except
think of you. Watched hockey on TV. I hate that new
thing they're doing with that little blue fuzzy spot
that follows the puck around the ice on your TV
screen. It reminds me of those asinine circles John
Madden draws on the screen while he's blabbering
about football games. Cripes. If you can't keep your
eye on the puck then you shouldn't be watching
hockey, for Chrissakes.

I wondered what you were doing today. Did you work
at home on your computer while Gary putzed around
the house? Did you go outside and make angels in
the snow? (I don't even know where you live—is
there snow where you are, too?) Or did you curl up
with a good book and an afghan and a cat on your
lap and have one of those Maxwell House Moments?

Max

> Private Mail
> Date: Monday, February 5, 1996 6:19 p.m.
> From: Maximilian@miller&morris.com
> Subj: Crazy
> To: BevJ@frederic_gerard.com

Bev,

You must think I'm crazy because I keep writing to you, even though you never respond. Maybe I am a little crazy. You make me crazy. Or I make myself crazy. But I'm not going to stop writing to you. Sometimes I tell myself that I don't care if you never respond to my messages—that just being able to talk to you through e-mail and share parts of my life with you is enough.

Then I'll fire up my computer at work in the morning, and while I'm popping open my first diet Coke of the day and waiting for the computer to boot and my telecom program to launch, in the back of my mind I think maybe, just maybe, there'll be a message from her. I stare at the computer screen, and when it says I have a message waiting, I hold my breath and wonder what it is you're finally going to say to me and how should I respond—should I act casual, maybe wait a few days before I answer your message? Pay you back for all the times you've made me wait? Or should I reply right away, and tell you once again how much I love you and how happy I am to know that yes, you've been receiving and even reading all of my messages?

I don't realize how rigidly I'm sitting in my chair or how far I'm leaning forward, holding the can of Coke to my lips, riveted to the screen, watching that stupid little pendulum swing back and forth as I'm waiting for the message to download.

It's from dick@miller&morris.com and he's decided that the Macintosh is dead and that all the writers and designers in the ad agency must immediately dispose of their Macs and learn how to use PCs by the end of this week.

Bosses. Gotta love 'em.

Max

> Private Mail
> Date: Saturday, February 10, 1996 2:48 a.m.
> From: Maximilian@miller&morris.com
> Subj: First Class
> To: BevJ@frederic_gerard.com

So there's this blonde woman and she's sitting in the First Class section of an airplane, even though her ticket says she's supposed to be in Coach. The stewardess (oops, I mean flight attendant) walks up to her and says, "Ma'am, I'm sorry, but your ticket isn't for First Class so you're going to have to take your seat in the Coach section." To which the blonde woman replies, "I'm blonde; I'm smart; I have a good job; and I'm staying in this seat until the plane reaches Jamaica."

So the flight attendant goes and gets the head flight attendant, and the head flight attendant says to the blonde woman, "Ma'am, your ticket is for Coach, not First Class, and so you really must go sit in the Coach section now." To which the blonde woman replies, "I'm blonde; I'm smart; I have a good job; and I'm staying in this seat until the plane reaches Jamaica."

The two flight attendants go get the co-pilot and tell him what's going on. The co-pilot then walks over to the blonde woman, leans over, and whispers something in her ear. The blonde woman promptly gets out of her First Class seat and goes and sits in the Coach section. Amazed, the flight attendants ask the co-pilot what he whispered in her ear, and he says, "I told her that the front half of the plane wasn't going to Jamaica."

Max

> Private Mail
> Date: Wednesday, February 14, 1996 11:44 p.m.
> From: Maximilian@miller&morris.com
> Subj: Green Things
> To: BevJ@frederic_gerard.com

Beverly,

I had a date tonight. Are you jealous? Her name is Steffanee—not Stephanie—isn't that cute? (She wants me to call her Steffee.) She works for one of those plant services, where they send people out to high-rise office buildings every day to water the plants, wipe the dust off the leaves, put those little fertilizer sticks in the dirt, and stuff like that. They all wear yellow polo shirts with a picture of a flower in a pot with a smiley face in the middle of the flower embroidered in green on the pocket of the shirt, and they walk around with these little spritzer bottles clipped to their belts. Steffee works on my floor on Wednesdays. She even wears a yellow and green baseball cap that matches the shirt.

Anyhow, she's kind of cute, and everyone in the office always teases me about the plants in my office being the shiniest in the whole building. I guess that's because Steffee makes extra certain my plants are in tippee toppee shape.

It was about 4:30 and Steffee's in my office picking the dead leaves off my Benjamin Ficus, and I'm thinking about how it's Valentine's Day, that I have nothing better to do, and that pretty soon she's going to run out of dead leaves to pick—or maybe she'll just start picking off the green ones, because I'm sitting there at my desk smiling dreamily at her and she knows I'm watching. So right before she plucks off the last brown leaf I ask her if she'll have dinner with me, and she says yes of course, but she'll have to go home and change first and could I pick her up at six? I say yeah, sure, and ask her where she lives, and even though I'm sitting at my desk and there's scraps of paper all over the place, she takes the

Sharpie marker out of my Carpe Diem coffee mug
and writes her address and phone number in real big
letters on the inside of my forearm. I'm thinking
maybe this Valentine's Day isn't going to be so bad
after all.

Neither of us was in the mood for anything fancy so
we ended up at a delicatessen near Steffee's apart-
ment. Most of the women I've gone out with order a
salad on the first date. I hate that. What do they
think? That they're going to fool me into thinking
they eat salads all the time? Especially because like,
by the fourth or fifth date, we'll go to the movies
and while I'm enjoying a box of Junior Mints, the
woman who daintily picked at her salad on our first
date is now snarfing down the jumbo-size bucket of
popcorn with extra butter. So I was pleasantly surprised when Steffee ordered a salami on rye, extra
chips, and an entire dill pickle. Even more surprised
when she ate it all, too. The dill pickle finale was
especially entertaining.

Happy Valentine's Day, my love.

Maximilian

2   1   **2**
            3
5   4   5
7   7   8

> Private Mail
> Date: Thursday, February 15, 1996 8:45 a.m.
> From: BevJ@frederic_gerard.com
> Subj: You Idiot
> To: Maximilian@miller&morris.com

Maximilian,

Never, EVER, call me on the telephone again.

What were you thinking? And how did you find me? No, don't answer that. I don't want to know. I want you to promise me that you will never call my office again. I can only thank my lucky stars that my home phone number is unlisted. If you ever call me at the office again, I'll quit my job. Then you'll never be able to find me. And just to make double-sure, I'll change my name, join the Federal Witness Protection Program, *and* have a sex-change operation.

Beverly

> Private Mail
> Date: Thursday, February 15, 1996 2:26 p.m.
> From: Maximilian@miller&morris.com
> Subj: You Idiot
> To: BevJ@frederic_gerard.com

Bev,

Omigod. I feel terrible. I can't believe I did such a stupid thing. I think it was a build-up of my frustration over not hearing from you all these months. Everything just bubbled over, Bev.

After I came home from my date with Steffee last night and wrote you that message, I started knocking back more martinis. I was getting really polluted when it suddenly occurred to me out of nowhere that I might be able to figure out your work phone number from the domain name in your e-mail address. On a whim I typed http://www.frederic_gerard.com into my Web browser and there it was! Welcome to the Frederic Gerard Publishing Company World Wide Web Site!!! You guys make it pretty hard to find any of the editors' names on the Web site, but at least I was able to find a phone number for your main switchboard. So I copied down the number and decided to stay up drinking all night, waiting for morning and for your switchboard to open.

When the operator answered and I asked to speak to Beverly, she asked me for your last name and I couldn't remember it. (I obviously wasn't thinking clearly. I know your last name from those live COs on the Writer's Forum.) I told her I was returning your call and that I couldn't read my secretary's handwriting on the message slip. (Like anybody even uses those pink "While You Were Out" message pads anymore—doesn't your receptionist know everyone uses e-mail now?) So she puts me through, and I about fell off my chair when you picked up on the first ring and said, "This is Beverly."

I hadn't thought about what I was going to say—or even if I was going to say anything at all. Maybe I was thinking that I could just listen to your voice on your voice-mail message, "Hello. You've reached the voice mail of the incredibly sexy Bev Johnson. I'm either on the phone or away from my desk right now, so please leave a message and I'll call you back." BEEEP. Or, if you did pick up the phone, I thought maybe I would just sit there and listen to you saying, "This is Beverly....Hello? HelLOoo...." and then listen to you hang up after another moment of puzzled silence. But when you finally said, "Who the fuck is this?" after a few seconds of dead air (instead of just hanging up the phone, like a normal person would do) I couldn't help but laugh and tell you it was me.

I mean, come on, Bev. How many people would say "Who the fuck is this?" when they really have no idea who's on the other end of the line? It could have been your boss, for cryin' out loud!

Or did you know it was me?

Whatever. I just want to tell you that I'm sorry, that I promise to never call you at the office again, and that I still think you're a real piece of work.

Max

> Private Mail
> Date: Sunday, February 18, 1996 1:19 a.m.
> From: Maximilian@miller&morris.com
> Subj: Still Hungry
> To: BevJ@frederic_gerard.com

Bev. Don't go checking out on me now. Do you mean to tell me that after all this time, you're going to let it end like this? You send me one message telling me to never call you again and you think I'm just going to slither away like a hungry caterpillar?

Maximilian

> Private Mail
> Date: Monday, February 26, 1996 7:02 a.m.
> From: BevJ@frederic_gerard.com
> Subj: Still Hungry
> To: Maximilian@miller&morris.com

Maximilian,

No, I'm not checking out on you. I'm just trying to
decide what to say next.

Beverly

> Private Mail
> Date: Monday, February 26, 1996 10:18 a.m.
> From: Maximilian@miller&morris.com
> Subj: Still Hungry
> To: BevJ@frederic_gerard.com

Bev,

I'm glad you're not going to let us end this way. And
here's a little suggestion on what you should say
next. Feel free to simply copy and paste the follow-
ing message into your next reply. <weg>

Max

******************Cut Here***********************

My Dearest Max,

I am deeply sorry for ignoring you all these months.
I would never have chosen to ignore you voluntarily
but my mean old husband had me chained up in the
attic all this time so I couldn't answer your e-mail
messages.

Now that I am free I want to tell you how very much
I love you and what a wonderful man you are, and to
beg your forgiveness for my silence of the previous
months.

Your Darling Bev

******************Cut Here***********************

> Private Mail
> Date: Friday, March 1, 1996 7:59 a.m.
> From: BevJ@frederic_gerard.com
> Subj: Har Dee Har Har
> To: Maximilian@miller&morris.com

Get real, Maximilian. That's not even close to what I
was going to say.

Beverly

> Private Mail
> Date: Saturday, March 2, 1996 2:47 p.m.
> From: Maximilian@miller&morris.com
> Subj: Har Dee Har Har
> To: BevJ@frederic_gerard.com

So then. What *were* you going to say?

Max

> Private Mail
> Date: Monday, March 4, 1996 5:11 a.m.
> From: BevJ@frederic_gerard.com
> Subj: Two Conditions
> To: Maximilian@miller&morris.com

I was going to say that I'll correspond with you
again—under two conditions.

Beverly

> Private Mail
> Date: Monday, March 4, 1996 8:02 a.m.
> From: Maximilian@miller&morris.com
> Subj: Two Conditions
> To: BevJ@frederic_gerard.com

And they are?

Max

> Private Mail
> Date: Thursday, March 7, 1996 8:02 a.m.
> From: BevJ@frederic_gerard.com
> Subj: Two Conditions
> To: Maximilian@miller&morris.com

The first condition is that we only talk by e-mail—
no phone calls.

Beverly

> Private Mail
> Date: Thursday, March 7, 1996 9:58 a.m.
> From: Maximilian@miller&morris.com
> Subj: Two Conditions
> To: BevJ@frederic_gerard.com

I've already promised you that. What's the second
condition?

Max

> Private Mail
> Date: Monday, March 11, 1996 7:20 a.m.
> From: BevJ@frederic_gerard.com
> Subj: Two Conditions
> To: Maximilian@miller&morris.com

The second condition is that we talk to each other

only as friends—no romantic stuff. The thing that happened at Macworld was a one-time thing, and I would like for you to promise me that you'll never bring it up again.

Beverly

> Private Mail
> Date: Monday, March 11, 1996 12:03 p.m.
> From: Maximilian@miller&morris.com
> Subj: Two Conditions
> To: BevJ@frederic_gerard.com

Bring *what* up again?

<g>

Max

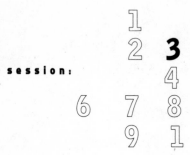

session:
1
2
3
4
6 7 8
9 1

> Private Mail
> Date: Wednesday, March 13, 1996 9:11 p.m.
> From: Maximilian@miller&morris.com
> Subj: Small Talk
> To: BevJ@frederic_gerard.com

Bev,

Now that we've got that squared away, what have you
been doing these past few months? Has life been
treating you well? How's work going?

Max

> Private Mail
> Date: Thursday, March 14, 1996 7:31 a.m.
> From: BevJ@frederic_gerard.com
> Subj: Small Talk
> To: Maximilian@miller&morris.com

Everything's been going great, Maximilian. I've been spending a lot of time on this project at work that has really captured my interest—we've started a new book series and I've been selected as the series editor. It's turning out to be a fun project and my publisher is giving me free rein to not only hire the best authors for each book, but offer them decent contracts for once, too. Which means we don't have to waste precious time mud-wrestling over contract details.

How about you? What have you been doing with your life—I mean, besides watching hockey, telling blonde jokes, and dating adolescent plant girls? ;-)

Beverly

> Private Mail
> Date: Thursday, March 14, 1996 12:53 p.m.
> From: Maximilian@miller&morris.com
> Subj: Small Talk
> To: BevJ@frederic_gerard.com

Cute, Bev.

Things here have been pretty good. Work has calmed down a bit—at least for the time being—because my boss has been traveling in Europe, so now we only have to deal with his tirades over the phone or via e-mail. I'm working on the copy for the new Olivia's Boutique catalog, and instead of just doing the copy-writing, I get to have some input at the photo shoots and on the layout. So yesterday I got to spend the day with our photographer in a room full of scantily clad fashion models.

Can we talk about things other than work?

Max

p.s. Let me know when the first book in your series comes out and I'll order it from Amazon.com.

> Private Mail
> Date: Monday, March 18, 1996 5:19 a.m.
> From: BevJ@frederic_gerard.com
> Subj: Small Talk
> To: Maximilian@miller&morris.com

Maximilian,

Of course we can talk about things other than work. As long as we keep the conversation within the boundaries of what two friends would talk about, I think we should be fine.

> Private Mail
> Date: Monday, March 18, 1996 11:26 a.m.
> From: Maximilian@miller&morris.com
> Subj: Small Talk
> To: BevJ@frederic_gerard.com

Bev,

So how's things with you and Gary?

Max

> Private Mail
> Date: Tuesday, March 19, 1996 7:03 a.m.
> From: BevJ@frederic_gerard.com
> Subj: Small Talk?
> To: Maximilian@miller&morris.com

Everything with Gary and me is just fine,
Maximilian. He had been putting in a lot of hours at
the office, so his company sent the two of us to the
Bahamas for a week in December. It was fabulous.

Beverly

> Private Mail
> Date: Wednesday, March 20, 1996 10:20 a.m.
> From: Maximilian@miller&morris.com
> Subj: Small Talk?
> To: BevJ@frederic_gerard.com

That's great, Bev. Really glad to hear it. Did you
stay on the main island?

Max

> Private Mail
> Date: Thursday, March 21, 1996 6:56 a.m.
> From: BevJ@frederic_gerard.com
> Subj: Baubles in Bimini
> To: Maximilian@miller&morris.com

No, actually we stayed on Bimini and drank
Goombay Smashes at the Compleat Angler every
night.

Beverly

> Private Mail
> Date: Friday, March 22, 1996 9:41 a.m.
> From: Maximilian@miller&morris.com
> Subj: Baubles in Bimini
> To: BevJ@frederic_gerard.com

Sounds marvy.

::: Sigh. :::

I guess there's not much else to talk about, then.

> Private Mail
> Date: Monday, March 25, 1996 8:02 a.m.
> From: BevJ@frederic_gerard.com
> Subj: Evergreen
> To: Maximilian@miller&morris.com

Well, how's things with you and the plant girl?

Beverly

> Private Mail
> Date: Monday, March 25, 1996 11:17 a.m.
> From: Maximilian@miller&morris.com
> Subj: Evergreen
> To: BevJ@frederic_gerard.com

Her name is Steffanee, Bev.

Max

> Private Mail
> Date: Tuesday, March 26, 1996 5:30 a.m.
> From: BevJ@frederic_gerard.com
> Subj: Evergreen
> To: Maximilian@miller&morris.com

Sure, Maximilian. Steffanee. Or shall I call her
Steffee?

Beverly

> Private Mail
> Date: Tuesday, March 26, 1996 10:12 a.m.
> From: Maximilian@miller&morris.com
> Subj: Evergreen
> To: BevJ@frederic_gerard.com

What is it exactly you'd like to know, Beverly? Yes, I'm still seeing her, and yes, I'm enjoying her company. She's a nice girl—she's even going back to school to finish her degree.

Maximilian

> Private Mail
> Date: Tuesday, March 26, 1996 12:40 p.m.
> From: BevJ@frederic_gerard.com
> Subj: Evergreen
> To: Maximilian@miller&morris.com

Oh, you mean she's already graduated from high school?

Beverly

> Private Mail
> Date: Tuesday, March 26, 1996 1:16 p.m.
> From: Maximilian@miller&morris.com
> Subj: Evergreen
> To: BevJ@frederic_gerard.com

You're a riot, Alice.

Seriously—what is it that you want to know?

Maximilian

> Private Mail
> Date: Wednesday, March 27, 1996 7:21 a.m.
> From: BevJ@frederic_gerard.com
> Subj: Evergreen
> To: Maximilian@miller&morris.com

Nevermind.

session: **4**

> Private Mail
> Date: Thursday, March 28, 1996 6:02 a.m.
> From: BevJ@frederic_gerard.com
> Subj: The Real Thing
> To: Maximilian@miller&morris.com

Maximilian:

Do you really drink diet Coke in the morning? That's kind of gross, don't you think? I thought you told me once when we were chatting that you were drinking coffee.

Beverly

> Private Mail
> Date: Thursday, March 28, 1996 10:52 a.m.
> From: Maximilian@miller&morris.com
> Subj: Some like it cold
> To: BevJ@frederic_gerard.com

Bev,

I'm on my third diet Coke today, as a matter of fact.
I usually pop open a can after I get out of the shower
in the morning, have another one on the train on my
way to work, and another diet Coke once I get set-
tled in at the office.

What's so gross about drinking diet Coke in the
morning? Some people like their caffeine hot; I hap-
pen to like mine cold. I do drink a cup of coffee on
the weekends once in a while—especially when I'm
nursing a particularly bad hangover. But most of the
time I prefer the lovely little caramel-colored bub-
bles you can only get from a can of Coke.

Max

p.s. So you *were* reading all of my messages! ;-)

> Private Mail
> Date: Friday, March 29, 1996 7:44 a.m.
> From: BevJ@frederic_gerard.com
> Subj: Some like it hot
> To: Maximilian@miller&morris.com

Maximilian,

Yes, I read all of your messages. I saved them, too.

Usually I drink a large black Kona Blend when I get
to the office, but on Fridays I treat myself to a large
cafe mocha with whipped cream and chocolate sprin-
kles on top. We have one of those trendy little coffee
shops on the first floor of our building. I've been
going there every day since it opened, and the same
girl with a nose ring and black fingernail polish has
been working behind the counter for three years now.
She always pretends like she's never seen me before.
I don't get it. Every morning she asks, "Can I help
you?" and every morning (except Friday) I tell her I'd
like a large Kona Blend. Then she asks me if I'd like
regular or decaf, and I always say regular. She gives
me the coffee, and then she says, "Anything else with
that?" and I say no thanks, just like I always do.
Then on Fridays, when I ask for the cafe mocha
instead of the Kona Blend, she acts surprised, as if
she was expecting me to ask for the Kona Blend. So I
know she knows that I'm the person who usually gets
the large Kona Blend. And yet come Monday morning when I walk in the door of that place, she invari-
ably says, "Can I help you?" as if she's never seen me
before.

Just once I'd like to be able to walk into that goddamned place and have her say, "Good morning.
Large Kona Blend?" or "Hello. Will you be having
your regular this morning?"

> Private Mail
> Date: Monday, April 1, 1996 10:02 a.m.
> From: Maximilian@miller&morris.com
> Subj: Some like it hot
> To: BevJ@frederic_gerard.com

Bev,

Good morning. Large Kona Blend?

Love,
Max

p.s. Did you really save all of the messages I wrote to
you? Does that mean you still have them? Aren't you
worried about Gary finding them?

> Private Mail
> Date: Monday, April 1, 1996 11:12 a.m.
> From: BevJ@frederic_gerard.com
> Subj: Some like it hot
> To: Maximilian@miller&morris.com

<smile>

This morning I decided to really shift the nose-ring
girl's paradigm. I ordered orange juice and a banana
muffin instead of the large Kona Blend.

Bev

p.s. Yes, I really did save your messages, and yes, I still have all of them, and no, I'm not worried about Gary finding them—he's not the kind of guy to go snooping around on my computer. Did you save any of my messages?

> Private Mail
> Date: Tuesday, April 2, 1996 6:47 p.m.
> From: Maximilian@miller&morris.com
> Subj: The Real Thing
> To: BevJ@frederic_gerard.com

What did the nose-ring girl do?

Max

p.s. I didn't save your messages at first, but I did begin saving them after I realized you were the one who... I mean, after we, uh, you know—after we did the thing that I'm not supposed to mention because it was just a "one-time thing."

> Private Mail
> Date: Wednesday, April 3, 1996 5:39 a.m.
> From: BevJ@frederic_gerard.com
> Subj: The Real Thing
> To: Maximilian@miller&morris.com

Max,

She freaked. I thought she was going to go postal on me. It was hilarious. I could've sworn I saw her hand reaching for the pot of Kona Blend at the very moment she was saying the words "Can I help you?" as if she had never seen me before, just like always. She had her back to the counter when I said, softly, that I'd like a small orange juice. She whipped her head around so fast I thought it was going to go flying off her shoulders! Then, after she gave me the juice and asked me if I'd like anything else with that, I smiled sweetly and said that yes, I would like a banana muffin too. I think that really pushed her over the edge.

I'm thinking of painting my fingernails black.

Bev

p.s. Aren't you worried that the plant girl—oops, I mean Steffanee—is going to find my messages?

> Private Mail
> Date: Wednesday, April 3, 1996 10:26 a.m.
> From: Maximilian@miller&morris.com
> Subj: The Real Thing
> To: BevJ@frederic_gerard.com

That is a great story, Bev! But don't paint your fingernails black. I like your hands just the way they are.

And, to answer your question, no, I'm not worried about Steffee finding the messages. It's not like she and I are living together or anything.

Max

p.s. I know I'm not supposed to bring it up, but do you ever think about the night we were together?

> Private Mail
> Date: Thursday, April 4, 1996 8:33 a.m.
> From: BevJ@frederic_gerard.com
> Subj: The Real Thing
> To: Maximilian@miller&morris.com

Yes, all the time.

session: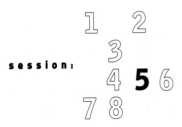

>Thursday, April 11, 7:01 p.m.

> Writer's Forum   > Live Conference   > People Here: 28

DonA(Mod): Hello everyone, and thank you for join-
ing tonight's live conference here on
the Writer's Forum. For those of you
who've just joined us, the topic of
tonight's chat is How to Write a
Query Letter: what to say and what not
to say when you first approach a book
editor or agent. Our guest speaker
tonight is Beverly Johnson, editor-in-
chief at Frederic Gerard Publishing.

Before we get started I'd like to briefly go over a few of the rules of live conference etiquette...If you'd like to ask a question, type a ? (question mark) or, if you'd like to make a comment, type an ! (exclamation point). As the moderator, I'll tell you to go ahead with a "GA" followed by your name. If you all behave yourselves and refrain from asking Bev questions like the guy in Bev's last conference, who asked her what color underwear she's wearing, I won't have to interject too much. :-)

Beverly, can you start by explaining to us exactly what a query letter is and why it's so important?

BevJ: Thanks Don, and hello everyone. A query is a short introductory letter sent to a publisher or agent that briefly describes your manuscript or proposal. It's part of a query package that will include supporting materials such as an author bio, a sample of your previously published work, and a synopsis of your book. The immediate goal of the query letter is to pique the person's interest enough so that he or she will turn the page and read the rest of the materials in the package. The ultimate goal of the query package is to get the editor or agent interested enough in your book project so that he or she asks to see more, such as a sample chapter and an outline, or in the case of fiction, the entire manuscript.

The query letter is like an advertisement in that it must convey your message in an instant. It must be well-presented and easy to read. Yet the query must also be substantive, demonstrating that your idea is well thought-out and well researched. It should also demonstrate your skills as a writer.

CraigK: ?

DonA(Mod):   GA, CraigK.

CraigK: Beverly, what sorts of things should an author *not* include in a query letter?

DonA(Mod):   GA, Bev.

BevJ: That's a good question, Craig. One of the things that an author should definitely try to avoid when writing a query letter is describing the book using superlatives. In other words, don't say that your manuscript is "absolutely fabulous" or "a real winner"—leave that sort of judgment to the agent or editor, and stick to describing your manuscript in terms of its content and marketability.

RickW: ?

DonA(Mod):   GA, Rick.

RickW: Bev, I've read that the query letter should always be limited to one page. Do you agree with that, and is there ever a time when a longer query letter is appropriate?

DonA(Mod): GA, Bev.

BevJ: If at all possible, Rick, the author should certainly try to limit the query to one page. I've seen a few good queries that were two pages, but they were the exception. To keep the query down to one page, you can include the supporting materials I mentioned above, such as a bio and a synopsis, as separate documents. But, as I said, the query letter itself is like an ad, in that your immediate goal is to get the editor's attention, capturing her interest long enough that she'll read to the bottom of the page. In that amount of space, you should be able to say what your book is about, describe your basic qualifications as a writer, and provide a brief analysis of the marketability and unique benefits of your book. And don't forget to end your letter with an invitation to request further material, as well as a "thank-you."

elyse: ?

Maximilian: !

DonA(Mod): GA, elyse, then GA, Maximilian.

elyse: Beverly, does it matter what kind of stationery you use for your query?

BevJ: There are no specific requirements for stationery, elyse, as long as your presentation is tasteful and readable. A few publishers (though not many) accept e-mail queries, so in that case you don't have to worry about paper and postage. If you send your query via snail mail, however, remember to include a SASE (self-addressed, stamped envelope) with your query so the agent or editor can return your materials along with a response.

Maximilian: Hi Bev...

BevJ: Hello, Maximilian.

Maximilian: What's the best way to start off a query letter?

BevJ: Well, there are no hard and fast rules about exactly what you should say in the first sentence, Max, but I will say don't say something outrageous that has nothing to do with your proposal just to get the editor's attention, and do try to be positive and upbeat.

Maximilian: You mean you shouldn't start a query with something like, "FREE SEX MONEY SEX FREE SEX!!!" or "My book idea has been rejected by 34 editors so far and if you don't ask to see my manuscript I'm gonna commit hara kiri"?

BevJ: Neither of those would be a good way to start the query, Max—unless your book really is a how-to guide for committing hara kiri, or tells people where to find unlimited amounts of free sex and money. <g>

Maximilian: One more question, Bev—what color underwear are you wearing?

	JUST KIDDING!!! <weg>
BevJ:	:::slap!:::
DonA(Mod):	OK Max, let's get back on topic here. I think we have just enough time for one more question.
Netman:	?
DonA(Mod):	GA, Netman.
Netman:	Beverly, does your company publish computer books? I'm not a writer but I'm a network manager who's been on the Internet for a number of years and I have an idea for an Internet book.
BevJ:	As a matter of fact, Frederic Gerard does publish computer books, Netman, although as far as Internet books go, the market is somewhat glutted right now. There are nearly 600 Internet-related titles currently on the shelves, with more to come. But if you'd like to send me a brief query via e-mail I'd be happy to take a look at your idea. You don't always have to be the first to market to be the best.
Netman:	That's great, Beverly! Thank you. :-)
BevJ:	You're welcome, Netman.
DonA(Mod):	I'm sorry we've run out of time for more questions. I'd like to thank Beverly Johnson of Frederic Gerard Publishing for joining us tonight, and audience members, you're welcome to stick around for an informal,

	unmoderated discussion now that the conference is over. Everyone into the pool!
BevJ:	Thanks for inviting me here tonight, Don. Ciao everyone!
	:::waving goodbye:::
RickW:	Goodnight Bev!
elyse:	Thanks Beverly!
%System%:	BevJ has left the forum.
Netman:	So, do you think Beverly will really read my query letter?
elyse:	She's been in the publishing business a long time, Netman, and I hear she does read and respond to every e-mail query she gets.
RickW:	I heard from someone who used to work for her she's a real ball-buster.
Maximilian:	I've never worked for her, but I can vouch for that. ;-)

session:

6

1
2 3
4
7 8
9 1

> Private Mail
> Date: Friday, April 12, 1996 8:14 a.m.
> From: BevJ@frederic_gerard.com
> Subj: First Time for Everything
> To: Maximilian@miller&morris.com

Maximilian,

You never told me about your first kiss.

Beverly

> Private Mail
> Date: Sunday, April 14, 1996 2:03 a.m.
> From: Maximilian@miller&morris.com
> Subj: First Time for Everything
> To: BevJ@frederic_gerard.com

Bev,

You never told me what kind of underwear you wear.

Max

> Private Mail
> Date: Monday, April 15, 1996 7:59 a.m.
> From: BevJ@frederic_gerard.com
> Subj: First Time for Everything
> To: Maximilian@miller&morris.com

But now you already know that.

> Private Mail
> Date: Monday, April 15, 1996 10:11 a.m.
> From: Maximilian@miller&morris.com
> Subj: First Time for Everything
> To: BevJ@frederic_gerard.com

Wellll, I at least know what kind of underwear you
were wearing on the night I'm not supposed to talk
about. Do you always wear underwear that, um,
sexy—like, even to work and stuff?

> Private Mail
> Date: Wednesday, April 17, 1996 8:08 a.m.
> From: BevJ@frederic_gerard.com
> Subj: We're not really talking about this
> To: Maximilian@miller&morris.com

Yeah, sure. Why not?

You know, you tell me I'm a real piece of work, but I think you're the one who's a piece of work. I start out asking you a question and all of a sudden we're talking about my underwear.

Bev

p.s. You're also talking about the night we're not supposed to talk about, and I think we should cease and desist immediately.

> Private Mail
> Date: Thursday, April 18, 1996 6:47 p.m.
> From: Maximilian@miller&morris.com
> Subj: Yes we are
> To: BevJ@frederic_gerard.com

I can think of nothing I'd rather discuss than your underwear. No, there is something I'd rather discuss—except you want me to stop talking about it.

Max

p.s. OK, I'll stop talking about it. But it *was* wonderful, wasn't it? }:-)

> Private Mail
> Date: Friday, April 19, 1996 5:58 a.m.
> From: BevJ@frederic_gerard.com
> Subj: No we're not
> To: Maximilian@miller&morris.com

Yes, it was.

So tell me about your first kiss.

Beverly

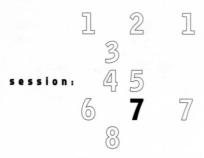

session:

> Private Mail
> Date: Monday, April 22, 1996 11:01 a.m.
> From: Maximilian@miller&morris.com
> Subj: First Kiss
> To: BevJ@frederic_gerard.com

Bev,

I was twelve and her name was Cindy Kriechbaum. I
really don't remember that much about it, except that
I was nervous and it was more weird than exciting.
She lived on my block and we were in back of my
school when it happened. (She went to the Catholic
school; I was a "public.") I'd been wanting to kiss her
for a long time, mostly because she had red hair

exactly like Ann-Margret's, who was a major source of inspiration for my fantasies at the time.

Max

> Private Mail
> Date: Tuesday, April 23, 1996 7:33 a.m.
> From: BevJ@frederic_gerard.com
> Subj: First Kiss
> To: Maximilian@miller&morris.com

Max,

Did you really fantasize about Ann-Margret when you were 12? Anyone else?

Beverly

> Private Mail
> Date: Tuesday, April 23, 1996 10:11 a.m.
> From: Maximilian@miller&morris.com
> Subj: First Fantasies
> To: BevJ@frederic_gerard.com

Bev,

I was hot for Ann. I thought I would die when I saw her in Viva! Las Vegas with Elvis Presley. She was so . . . perky. }:-)

Raquel Welch was also pretty hot at the time—she and Ann-Margret are *still* hot, IMO. A few years later my friends and I were really into Cheryl Tiegs—we all had the picture of her on the cover of the swimsuit issue of Sports Illustrated tacked to the ceiling above our beds. I remember Farrah Fawcett was popular around then, too, but she wasn't my type.

How about you—whom did you fantasize about?

Max

> Private Mail
> Date: Wednesday, April 24, 1996 6:56 a.m.
> From: BevJ@frederic_gerard.com
> Subj: First Fantasies
> To: Maximilian@miller&morris.com

I had a huge crush on both Batman and Robin when I was, like, 10 or 11. I swear I had never heard of a ménage à trois at the time, but my first sexual fantasies involved both masked men. <weg>

Donny Osmond had me going for a while, but not for long. My mom bought me the album with Donny's face all over the front (the one with Puppy Love on it). I also had a Partridge Family album. But I quickly outgrew them and graduated to my lifelong fascination with Elvis, which began when I was about 13 and is still going strong today. Although I

didn't go to high school with Elvis, I'm convinced
that had he taken *me* to the senior prom, he would
still be alive today.

Bev

> Private Mail
> Date: Wednesday, April 24, 1996 10:51 a.m.
> From: Maximilian@miller&morris.com
> Subj: Holy Three-Ways, Batman!
> To: BevJ@frederic_gerard.com

Wow! You were quite the precocious young lady,
there, Bev. Batman *and* Robin at the same time?
Where do you come up with these things? And have
you thought of becoming a Hollywood screenwriter?

Max

p.s. You mean to tell me you actually think Elvis is
dead?

> Private Mail
> Date: Thursday, April 25, 1996 6:11 a.m.
> From: BevJ@frederic_gerard.com
> Subj: Holy Three-Ways, Batman!
> To: Maximilian@miller&morris.com

Speaking of becoming a Hollywood screenwriter, a

girlfriend of mine and I have an idea to produce a
line of erotic videos especially for women. Every
porno movie we've ever seen is so stupid, so boring.
We've dreamed up a plan to write and produce x-
rated videos that women would enjoy watching. I
doubt we'll ever get around to it, though, since we're
both so busy with other things. Maybe someday.

Bev

p.s. I liked your message header, btw.

p.p.s. I don't *think* Elvis is dead—I *know* he's
dead. It said so in The National Enquirer. <g>

> Private Mail
> Date: Thursday, April 25, 1996 1:22 p.m.
> From: Maximilian@miller&morris.com
> Subj: Holy Three-Ways, Batman!
> To: BevJ@frederic_gerard.com

So, do you and your girlfriends spend a lot of time
together, um, watching porno movies??? <g,d&rvvf>

Max

> Private Mail
> Date: Friday, April 26, 1996 6:11 a.m.
> From: BevJ@frederic_gerard.com
> Subj: Holy Three-Ways, Batman!
> To: Maximilian@miller&morris.com

Max,

No, actually. The friend with whom I had the idea
for the erotic videos was one of my college room-
mates. We would go to the movies that they showed
on weeknights in college classrooms—you know, old
movies like Psycho, held as fundraisers by various
campus organizations where they charged a buck, a
buck-fifty to get in. (This was in the olden days,
before VCRs were in widespread use. <g>) One night
we got up the nerve to go see Deep Throat with a
bunch of other girls. We didn't want anyone to rec-
ognize us so we all wore brown paper bags over our
heads, with cutouts for the eyes. That movie was so
disgusting! We couldn't understand why guys liked it
so much. Well, we *could* understand, but we still
thought it was gross. So we started talking about
how we could make a much better x-rated movie that
women would actually enjoy watching.

Bev

> Private Mail
> Date: Friday, April 26, 1996 3:18 p.m.
> From: Maximilian@miller&morris.com
> Subj: Holy Three-Ways, Batman!
> To: BevJ@frederic_gerard.com

And do you care to share any of the plot details of
this x-rated video with your buddy Max? <weg>

> Private Mail
> Date: Friday, April 26, 1996 6:20 p.m.
> From: BevJ@frederic_gerard.com
> Subj: Zipless Fuck
> To: Maximilian@miller&morris.com

I think I already did, once.

session:

> Private Mail
> Date: Monday, April 29, 1996 6:36 a.m.
> From: BevJ@frederic_gerard.com
> Subj: Computers
> To: Maximilian@miller&morris.com

Max,

So. Did you ever figure out which Macintosh you're
going to buy?

Bev

> Private Mail
> Date: Monday, April 29, 1996 11:19 a.m.
> From: Maximilian@miller&morris.com
> Subj: Safe Topics
> To: BevJ@frederic_gerard.com

Bev,

Ah, changing the subject, are we? ;-)

Max

> Private Mail
> Date: Tuesday, April 30, 1996 8:02 a.m.
> From: BevJ@frederic_gerard.com
> Subj: Computers
> To: Maximilian@miller&morris.com

Maximilian,

No, that's not what I was doing. I was just thinking
about the first time you wrote to me asking my
advice on which computer you should buy, and you
mentioned in one of your messages a few months ago
that you still hadn't decided which Mac you were
going to get. So I was just wondering if you ever did
buy a Mac or not.

That's all—nothing more, nothing less.

Beverly

> Private Mail
> Date: Tuesday, April 30, 1996 10:27 a.m.
> From: Maximilian@miller&morris.com
> Subj: Safe Topics
> To: BevJ@frederic_gerard.com

Sure, Bev—whatever you say. <g>

Max

> Private Mail
> Date: Wednesday, May 1, 1996 6:16 a.m.
> From: BevJ@frederic_gerard.com
> Subj: Computers
> To: Maximilian@miller&morris.com

Maximilian:

Did anyone ever tell you that you can be highly
annoying at times?

Beverly

> Private Mail
> Date: Wednesday, May 1, 1996 10:49 a.m.
> From: Maximilian@miller&morris.com
> Subj: Safe Topics
> To: BevJ@frederic_gerard.com

Oh, sure, all the time. My maniacal boss takes great pleasure in recounting my many character deficits in full detail to me—he especially likes doing it in front of my colleagues at the ad agency. But at least he's never excoriated me for a lack of fashion sense: Yesterday he fired our art director during the middle of a presentation because his socks didn't match.

Max

> Private Mail
> Date: Thursday, May 2, 1996 7:46 a.m.
> From: BevJ@frederic_gerard.com
> Subj: Color Me Crazy
> To: Maximilian@miller&morris.com

You're joking, right?

Beverly

> Private Mail
> Date: Thursday, May 2, 1996 1:22 p.m.
> From: Maximilian@miller&morris.com
> Subj: Color Me Crazy
> To: BevJ@frederic_gerard.com

No, not at all. We were presenting the mock-ups of a print campaign for a clothing line belonging to one of our biggest clients. We had been working on this idea for months, and Dick (that's my boss—the owner of the ad agency) had already chosen the preliminary sketches and copy from three other concepts we presented to him about a month ago. So we were really just taking a theme he had already approved and perfecting the idea before we showed it to the client at the end of this week.

Anyhow, Tuesday's meeting was supposed to be fairly routine, sort of a dry run where we'd show the mock-ups one more time to Dick before presenting them to the client on Friday. So we're in this meeting, and it's me (the head copywriter on the project), the art director, a couple of junior copywriters, two graphic designers, and the account exec. The account exec was letting our art director do the presentation, because the art director is usually pretty good at these things.

So Joel (that's the art director) is standing up at the easel with his fancy schmancy pointer—one of those pen laser lights—which he's using to direct our attention to various aspects of the oversized mock-up of the print ad. Joel is a pretty smooth guy, and a rather smooth dresser too, if I say so myself. His clothes are on the casual/preppie side. You can tell he takes great care in selecting his outfit each day. Even when we all wear jeans on Fridays, Joel's jeans look cleaner and spiffier than everyone else's.

So anyway, Joel is breezing through the presentation, and you can tell he's thinking that it's going pretty well, which in my opinion was the first strategic error on Joel's part. (See, even if you think a meeting is going well at Miller & Morris Advertising, you should definitely conceal the fact that you think so.) I could see Dick nodding his head enthusiastically at each of Joel's points, sort of egging him on. That was Warning 1.

At the end of Joel's presentation, there was a slight pause, and Dick started out his comments in a very soft and polite voice (Warning 2) and said, "Please forgive me, but..." which was Warning 3 and definitely a good sign that Joel was now up Shit Creek without a paddle. By this time Joel realized he's been caught in Dick's Crosshairs of the Day, and you can see he's kind of bracing himself for what's coming. I personally thought Joel's face had that deer-caught-in-the-headlights-of-an-oncoming-truck look.

But enough of the personal commentary. Dick says to Joel, "Please forgive me, Joel, but, who approved this idea?" and Joel says, "You did, Dick. Remember when we had the meeting about a month ago..." (Error 2). Meanwhile the rest of us sitting around the table are shitting bricks because we were all at that meeting and we know Dick approved the concept that Joel was now presenting, but that Joel has no chance in hell of convincing Dick of that fact. So Dick proceeds to explain to Joel what's wrong with the ad—in particular, the colors are all wrong and because this is a fashion ad the colors have to be exactly right and since Joel is the art director and he is the one who chose the colors, he must be color blind. Yes! Joel *is* color blind! Because look at his socks peeking out from between his loafers and his chinos! THEY DO NOT MATCH! (It was shocking—Joel actually did have two different-color socks on that day: one plum-colored argyle sock and the other more of a maroon, or wine-colored argyle.) WHAT KIND OF ART DIRECTOR WOULD WEAR SOCKS TO WORK THAT DON'T MATCH?

And that was the end of Joel.

Max

> Private Mail
> Date: Friday, May 3, 1996 8:17 a.m.
> From: BevJ@frederic_gerard.com
> Subj: Color Me Crazy
> To: Maximilian@miller&morris.com

So what are you going to do for today's presentation to the client?

Bev

> Private Mail
> Date: Friday, May 3, 1996 9:59 a.m.
> From: Maximilian@miller&morris.com
> Subj: Color Me Crazy
> To: BevJ@frederic_gerard.com

Bev,

We resuscitated one of the concepts that Dick had previously rejected (I think he described this one in particular as "despicable"), re-presented it to him last night, and he LOVED it. Said it was "absolutely brilliant." Coincidentally, this was the concept that Joel and the rest of us thought from the beginning was the best one out of the bunch.

So that's what we'll be presenting to the client in this afternoon's meeting.

Max

> Private Mail
> Date: Monday, May 6, 1996 6:40 a.m.
> From: BevJ@frederic_gerard.com
> Subj: Color Me Crazy
> To: Maximilian@miller&morris.com

And Joel?

> Private Mail
> Date: Monday, May 6, 1996 10:35 a.m.
> From: Maximilian@miller&morris.com
> Subj: Color Me Crazy
> To: BevJ@frederic_gerard.com

A bunch of us are helping him find a job at another agency. He shouldn't have too much of a problem; our main competition across town loves taking Dick's castoffs, since he has a tendency to fire the most talented people at the agency.

> Private Mail
> Date: Tuesday, May 7, 1996 7:59 a.m.
> From: BevJ@frederic_gerard.com
> Subj: Color Me Crazy
> To: Maximilian@miller&morris.com

That's good of you. And why is it that you keep hanging around that place? Wouldn't you be better off working at the agency across town, too?

> Private Mail
> Date: Tuesday, May 7, 1996 10:03 a.m.
> From: Maximilian@miller&morris.com
> Subj: Color Me Crazy
> To: BevJ@frederic_gerard.com

In my mind it's six of one, half a dozen of the other. I'd just be jumping out of the frying pan into the fire if I left this agency and went to another. (Full of cliches today, aren't I?) So I'll continue to bide my time here until I get fired or I find something better to do—whichever comes first. Maybe someday I'll write a book.

> Private Mail
> Date: Wednesday, May 8, 1996 8:12 a.m.
> From: BevJ@frederic_gerard.com
> Subj: Color Me Crazy
> To: Maximilian@miller&morris.com

Is that why you were hanging out at the conference
the other night?

Bev

> Private Mail
> Date: Wednesday, May 8, 1996 9:41 a.m.
> From: Maximilian@miller&morris.com
> Subj: Color Me Crazy
> To: BevJ@frederic_gerard.com

Nah. That was just an excuse to be near you.

Max

session:

2
6
6 7
9
0

> Private Mail
> Date: Monday, May 13, 1996 5:42 a.m.
> From: BevJ@frederic_gerard.com
> Subj: Goodbye?
> To: Maximilian@miller&morris.com

Max,

I've been thinking about things for a few days and I
was thinking maybe we shouldn't talk to each other
anymore—or at least just cool it for a while.

Bev

> Private Mail
> Date: Monday, May 13, 1996 9:10 a.m.
> From: Maximilian@miller&morris.com
> Subj: Goodbye?
> To: BevJ@frederic_gerard.com

Why?

> Private Mail
> Date: Tuesday, May 14, 1996 7:50 a.m.
> From: BevJ@frederic_gerard.com
> Subj: Goodbye?
> To: Maximilian@miller&morris.com

Come on—you know why, Max.

Bev

> Private Mail
> Date: Tuesday, May 14, 1996 1:01 p.m.
> From: Maximilian@miller&morris.com
> Subj: Goodbye?
> To: BevJ@frederic_gerard.com

Because I annoy the hell out of you? <g>

Max

> Private Mail
> Date: Tuesday, May 14, 1996 4:53 p.m.
> From: BevJ@frederic_gerard.com
> Subj: Goodbye?
> To: Maximilian@miller&morris.com

<smile>

Precisely the opposite. I find myself thinking about
you more and more these days, not less. I thought at
first that we could keep in touch with each other and
still keep the relationship in check. But now I'm not
sure that's possible.

I enjoy your messages so much. I look forward to
hearing from you every day. On the days I don't get a
message from you, I feel disappointed. On the days I
do get a message from you, I go to bed at night com-
posing a reply to you in my mind.

It's not good for my marriage, Max. I know this must
seem crazy to you—all of this certainly seems crazy
to me—but I love Gary and I don't want to jeopar-
dize my relationship with him any more than I
already have. He's not stupid or unfeeling, Max. He's
a bright and caring and perceptive man. Even though
he's gone a lot because of his job, he's not blind. And
if we keep this up, sooner or later he's going to
notice that something's wrong—that I'm even more
preoccupied than I usually am. I don't want it to
come to that. And yet...I feel as if I'm becoming
addicted to you and your goddamned messages. We
should stop now while we still can.

> Private Mail
> Date: Wednesday, May 15, 1996 2:32 a.m.
> From: Maximilian@miller&morris.com
> Subj: Goodbye?
> To: BevJ@frederic_gerard.com

But it's not as if we're actually *doing* anything,
Bev. For Chrissakes, all we're doing is sending e-mail
messages to each other. I still don't even know where
you live—well, OK, I know where you work now and
I have a pretty good idea you must live somewhere in
the vicinity of your office. <g>

And, yeah, OK, we did sleep together once, but like
you said, it was a one-time thing and I've been doing
my best not to bring it up. It was an accident, really.
We didn't even know we were sleeping with each
other at the time it happened! Like you said, it was
in the Stupid Mistakes category; it was not something either of us would ever do again.

Max

> Private Mail
> Date: Wednesday, May 15, 1996 7:04 a.m.
> From: BevJ@frederic_gerard.com
> Subj: Stupid Mistake?
> To: Maximilian@miller&morris.com

But it *is* something I would do again, Max—that's
part of the problem. If it really was just a one-night
stand like I thought it would be—I worked so hard

to keep you from telling me your name that night—
then it would be so much easier to put it all behind
me. I thought I had pulled off the mother of all one-
night stands that night at Macworld last summer—
the whole thing was so unlike me, so spontaneous,
and yet so mysterious and exciting. I couldn't believe
I did what I did—invite a stranger to my room like
that.

And then it turns out that the stranger was you—
someone I had met online, someone I had begun to
share things with and trust, someone I had begun to
think of as my friend. Maybe I had even begun to
fall in love with the electronic version of you before
I made love with the physical you. I don't know.

Yes, I was mad as hell at you when I first found out
that you were the Goddamn Guy—the guy I had the
affair with. I was mad because you didn't tell me who
you were when I confided my secret to you and you
realized I was the one you had been with that night.
I felt foolish and embarrassed and humiliated.

Once I got over the embarrassment and the anger, I
was more scared than anything else. That's why I
didn't answer your messages for so long. I figured
that if I just ignored you, you would go away. I
thought I could eventually forget about you and
maybe even forgive myself for cheating on Gary like
that. I can't believe I did that to him. I *hate* myself
for that. But you kept persisting. You're so goddamned persistent, Max. You're like a dog chewin' on
a fucking bone.

But that's all beside the point. The point is that we
are doing something, Max. We keep sending each
other these crazy e-mails. Even though we may not
be anywhere near each other physically, we're occu-
pying each other's minds and hearts. When I talk
with you I feel like I *am* cheating on Gary, even
though I'm not actually cheating on him. Not really.
Not exactly. Well, sort of. Maybe. I think. A little
bit.

p.s. Did you mean it when you said being with me is
something you would never do again?

> Private Mail
> Date: Wednesday, May 15, 1996 9:17 a.m.
> From: Maximilian@miller&morris.com
> Subj: Stupid Mistake?
> To: BevJ@frederic_gerard.com

No, I was lying through my teeth when I said making
love with you is something I would never do again,
Bev. I would do it again in a New York minute. (And
I mean that both figuratively and literally—you get
me so worked up sometimes, I'm sure if I merely laid
eyes on you again I would immediately implode.)

Max

> Private Mail
> Date: Wednesday, May 15, 1996 5:28 p.m.
> From: BevJ@frederic_gerard.com
> Subj: TNT
> To: Maximilian@miller&morris.com

You mean explode.

Bev

> Private Mail
> Date: Wednesday, May 15, 1996 8:42 p.m.
> From: Maximilian@miller&morris.com
> Subj: TNT
> To: BevJ@frederic_gerard.com

What?

> Private Mail
> Date: Thursday, May 16, 1996 5:49 a.m.
> From: BevJ@frederic_gerard.com
> Subj: TNT
> To: Maximilian@miller&morris.com

You would explode, not implode, Max. Implode
means to burst inward, like a vacuum tube. If you
imploded that would be sort of gross. If you exploded, on the other hand, you would come to a sudden
violent point of release. I think in your case, explod-
ing would be preferable to imploding.

> Private Mail
> Date: Thursday, May 16, 1996 9:01 a.m.
> From: Maximilian@miller&morris.com
> Subj: TNT
> To: BevJ@frederic_gerard.com

OK, Webster. Whatever. If I saw you again I would explode, which, according to my dictionary, means that I would undergo rapid combustion with a sudden release of energy in the form of heat that causes violent expansion and consequent production of great disruptive pressure followed by a loud noise.

Max

> Private Mail
> Date: Thursday, May 16, 1996 4:44 p.m.
> From: BevJ@frederic_gerard.com
> Subj: TNT
> To: Maximilian@miller&morris.com

Which is exactly why I think we should quit talking to each other, Max. We're playing with fire here.

Bev

> Private Mail
> Date: Friday, May 17, 1996 1:23 a.m.
> From: Maximilian@miller&morris.com
> Subj: TNT
> To: BevJ@frederic_gerard.com

How about if we just cool it for a few days, like you said?

> Private Mail
> Date: Friday, May 17, 1996 7:36 a.m.
> From: BevJ@frederic_gerard.com
> Subj: TNT
> To: Maximilian@miller&morris.com

I didn't say "for a few days," Max. I think we should cool it for longer than that.

Bev

> Private Mail
> Date: Friday, May 17, 1996 9:08 a.m.
> From: Maximilian@miller&morris.com
> Subj: TNT
> To: BevJ@frederic_gerard.com

Like how long?

> Private Mail
> Date: Friday, May 17, 1996 11:48 a.m.
> From: BevJ@frederic_gerard.com
> Subj: TNT
> To: Maximilian@miller&morris.com

I don't know. Let me think about it.

session: 4 5
7 8
9 **10**
13
14

> Private Mail
> Date: Tuesday, May 21, 1996 3:18 a.m.
> From: Maximilian@miller&morris.com
> Subj: Happy Birthday to Me
> To: BevJ@frederic_gerard.com

Bev,

I know I'm supposed to be giving you a few days to
think about whatever it is you're thinking about, but
I just wanted to write and let you know that today
(well, yesterday—now that I notice it's after mid-
night) was my birthday.

Max

> Private Mail
> Date: Tuesday, May 21, 1996 7:12 a.m.
> From: BevJ@frederic_gerard.com
> Subj: Happy Birthday to You
> To: Maximilian@miller&morris.com

Happy Birthday, Max. I'm sorry I didn't know yesterday was your birthday. You didn't put a birth date on
your member profile. I do remember how old you are,
though. You just turned 33, right?

Did you have a good birthday?

Bev

> Private Mail
> Date: Tuesday, May 21, 1996 10:30 a.m.
> From: Maximilian@miller&morris.com
> Subj: Happy Birthday to Me
> To: BevJ@frederic_gerard.com

Oh yeah, I had a great birthday. Steffee and a bunch
of people from my office took me to this really crazy
restaurant where they have a New Orleans jazz band
and buckets of shrimp and the waiters and waitresses
do crude things like wear their underwear on the
outside of their clothing and blow up condoms with
helium and make balloons out of them. So I got a
bouquet of condoms and a bottle of Mad Dog 20/20
for my birthday.

Max

> Private Mail
> Date: Wednesday, May 22, 1996 8:11 a.m.
> From: BevJ@frederic_gerard.com
> Subj: Happy Birthday to You
> To: Maximilian@miller&morris.com

Were the condoms aquamarine, by chance? ;-)

Bev

p.s. Didn't you get anything else for your birthday,
like a present from Steffee or from someone in your
family?

> Private Mail
> Date: Wednesday, May 22, 1996 11:42 a.m.
> From: Maximilian@miller&morris.com
> Subj: Happy Birthday to Me
> To: BevJ@frederic_gerard.com

No, the condoms were clear, unfortunately. But they
also gave me a pack of those new talking condoms—
the ones where if you scratch your fingernail along
the strip on the outside of the package, it says
something, like "let's make love" in a really weird-
sounding voice.

My mom sent me some new shirts for work and
Steffee gave me a pen.

Max

> Private Mail
> Date: Thursday, May 23, 1996 6:27 a.m.
> From: BevJ@frederic_gerard.com
> Subj: Loquacious Latex?
> To: Maximilian@miller&morris.com

Oh—she gave you a new pen to replace the Sharpie marker that she uses to draw on your body parts with?

Haven't heard of the talking condoms. Amazing what they come up with these days.

Well, anyway. Happy Birthday.

Bev

> Private Mail
> Date: Thursday, May 23, 1996 9:17 a.m.
> From: Maximilian@miller&morris.com
> Subj: Birthday Wishes
> To: BevJ@frederic_gerard.com

Bev,

You know what I'd really like for my birthday?

Max

> Private Mail
> Date: Friday, May 24, 1996 7:15 a.m.
> From: BevJ@frederic_gerard.com
> Subj: Birthday Wishes
> To: Maximilian@miller&morris.com

Uh, lemme guess, Max. A talking diaphragm to go
with your talking condom?

Bev

> Private Mail
> Date: Friday, May 24, 1996 12:13 p.m.
> From: Maximilian@miller&morris.com
> Subj: Birthday Wishes
> To: BevJ@frederic_gerard.com

You're a real card, Bev. What I'd like is for you to
come spend the weekend with me.

Max

> Private Mail
> Date: Friday, May 24, 1996 3:36 p.m.
> From: BevJ@frederic_gerard.com
> Subj: Birthday Wishes
> To: Maximilian@miller&morris.com

You're out of your fucking mind, Max!

> Private Mail
> Date: Saturday, May 25, 1996 11:00 a.m.
> From: Maximilian@miller&morris.com
> Subj: Birthday Wishes
> To: BevJ@frederic_gerard.com

I had a feeling you'd say something along those lines.
It was worth a try, though, doncha think?

> Private Mail
> Date: Monday, May 27, 1996 10:23 a.m.
> From: BevJ@frederic_gerard.com
> Subj: Birthday Wishes
> To: Maximilian@miller&morris.com

What would you have done if I'd said yes, Max? I
think you were just huffing and puffing and blowing
a lot of smoke. I could have called your bluff, you
know.

> Private Mail
> Date: Monday, May 27, 1996 10:23 a.m.
> From: Maximilian@miller&morris.com
> Subj: Huffing & Puffing
> To: BevJ@frederic_gerard.com

So call my bluff, then, Bev. While I'm busy huffing
and puffing and bluffing, why don't you just get your
pretty little ass on a plane and come see me?

> Private Mail
> Date: Tuesday, May 28, 1996 6:48 a.m.
> From: BevJ@frederic_gerard.com
> Subj: Huffing & Puffing
> To: Maximilian@miller&morris.com

First off, I don't know where you live, Max, remember? And second I don't *want* to know where you
live. And furthermore it would be a very bad idea for
us to spend the weekend together.

This is why I want us to stop sending messages to
each other for a while—it's just getting too crazy.
Let's calm down, take a break, take a step back from
things, re-evaluate, stuff like that, OK?

Please.

Bev

> Private Mail
> Date: Tuesday, May 28, 1996 10:41 a.m.
> From: Maximilian@miller&morris.com
> Subj: Last Gasp
> To: BevJ@frederic_gerard.com

OK.

session:

1
4 1
16 6 7
8
9 **11**

> Thursday, July 11, 7:06 p.m.

> Writer's Forum   > Live Conference   > People Here: 31

DonA(Mod): Hello everyone, and thank you for
            joining tonight's live conference here
            on the Writer's Forum. For those of
            you who've just joined us, the topic of
            tonight's chat is Creativity: what it is
            and how to find it within ourselves.
            Our guest speaker is Maximilian
            Cortopassi, senior copywriter at Miller
            & Morris Advertising. Max is one of
            the creative minds behind the new
            Depot clothing ad campaign which has

been getting a lot of media attention the past few weeks. Max, thank you for taking time out of your busy schedule to talk with us. I'd like to start tonight's conference by asking: What is creativity?

Maximilian: Thanks for having me here, Don. In its simplest form, creativity is the ability to create—to make something, to bring something new into existence. In life, one of the most creative things a person can do is raise a child. A mother flying by the seat of her pants as she continually thinks of new ideas to make her children laugh, to help them grow, to keep them safe. That's creativity. In the advertising world, to be creative means to create something that's unconventional or unlike anything else that currently exists. Sometimes creativity is taking an old idea and implementing it in a new way. Creativity can manifest itself in many different forms.

JohnC: ?

DonA(Mod): GA, JohnC.

JohnC: Max, the Depot campaign works so well. How did you come up with the idea for the campaign?

Maximilian: Thank you, JC. The Depot ad campaign was a team effort. Like all of our campaigns at Miller & Morris, it started with a meeting with the client, the purpose of which was to learn the client's goals for the campaign. Were they interested in taking on the competition with a comparative ad? Were they introducing a new product? Were they trying to change the customer's mind about something, or generate sales leads? Were they trying to reinforce a previously established, successful campaign, or create an altogether new image? Once we figured out what the client wanted to accomplish, our creative team went to work brainstorming ideas. IMO, creativity in advertising is usually a result of good research. We've had this client for quite some time, so we didn't have to run out and do a whole bunch of research, but we did familiarize ourselves with the current marketplace before getting together for our brainstorming sessions.

Ann: ?

DonA(Mod): GA, Ann.

Ann: What makes for a good brainstorming session, Max? And, as a copywriter, do you prefer to work alone, or are you more creative in a group setting?

Maxmilian: I like to spend some time alone first thinking about the problem, getting to know the product—if it's something I can take home with me, I will. I'll use it, play with it, wear it. If it's edible, I'll eat it. Leo Burnett once said, "If you can't turn yourself into your customer, you probably shouldn't be in the advertising business at all." What he was talking about was empathy—the ability to see things from another person's point of view. If all of us on the team have developed a familiarity with the product and a certain degree of empathy for the customer, the brainstorming sessions tend to go pretty well.

Moe: ?

DonA(Mod): GA, Moe.

Moe: So how did you actually come up with the idea for the Depot ads?

Maximilian: It started with our art director, Joel, who's no longer with the agency, unfortunately. Joel is a pretty sharp dresser and when our team was assigned the campaign, he started wearing the client's clothing line to work, which is a little more casual than what he usually wears. Everyone started ribbing him about it and one time he shot back at us and said, "Hey, it takes confidence to be casual." And we all sort of looked at each other for half a minute—I could almost hear the gears in everyone's heads clanging at once—and we started jumping up and down saying, "That's it! That's it!" It was part serendipity and part research—the reason the idea clicked

	with all of us at once was because we had done our homework; I believe each of us already had a subconscious idea of the basic concept that would work best for this particular campaign.
KathyMc:	!
DonA(Mod):	GA, KathyMc.
KathyMc:	Hi Max...
Maximilian:	Hi Kathy. Nice to see you here. :-)
KathyMc:	The people you chose to model the clothing in the ads are gorgeous, Max. Why haven't you posed for one of the ads yourself? You'd be perfect. ;-)
Maximilian:	<blush> Why thanks, Kathy. I was too busy writing the copy and directing the photo shoots to be part of the ads. And besides, I'm too short to be a fashion model. <g>
KathyMc:	Saving yourself for the underwear ads, heh? <weg>
Maximilian:	No, actually I'm saving myself for the Ben & Jerry's ads. <g>
DonA(Mod):	OK guys, we're just about out of time. Max has been kind enough to offer his further thoughts on creativity as an uploaded text file to our Library here on the forum. It should be available and ready for downloading in the next 24 hours or so. Max, thanks again for being our guest tonight. Please feel free to stick around if you can for some informal chat. GA everyone!
Maximilian:	Thanks Don!
	::: stirring martini with index finger :::

BevJ:	Hi Max...
Maximilian:	<gasp> Look what the cat dragged in! <g> Hi Bev! Haven't seen you in a while...
KathyMc:	Hi Max.
Phil:	Hey Max! Great CO!
Maximilian:	Hi guys. Thanks Phil—glad you liked the conference. It was my first official guest appearance. Usually I simply butt in uninvited. <g>
KathyMc:	You were great, Max.
DonA(Mod):	Max, I've gotta run—will you send me that file via e-mail?
Maximilian:	Sure, Don. I'll send it to you in the morning.
KathyMc:	Goodnight, Max. Hope we see you here again soon!
Phil:	Bye Max.
JohnC:	Thanks Max!
Maximilian:	Bye everyone. Bev?
%System%:	BevJ has left the forum.
%System%:	Maximilian has left the forum.

session: **1 2**

> Private Mail
> Date: Monday, July 15, 1996 8:30 a.m.
> From: BevJ@frederic_gerard.com
> Subj: Good Job
> To: Maximilian@miller&morris.com

Hi Max,

You did a great job in last week's conference on creativity.

Beverly

> Private Mail
> Date: Wednesday, July 17, 1996 9:16 a.m.
> From: Maximilian@miller&morris.com
> Subj: Good Job
> To: BevJ@frederic_gerard.com

Thanks, Beverly. I was surprised to see you there. I haven't heard from you in almost two months.

Max

> Private Mail
> Date: Wednesday, July 17, 1996 11:28 a.m.
> From: BevJ@frederic_gerard.com
> Subj: Good Job
> To: Maximilian@miller&morris.com

Well, I saw the announcement about you being a conference guest on the "Today's News" splash screen—you know, the screen that pops up every morning when you first log on that has breaking news headlines, articles on current events, and blurbs about the day's online happenings. Anyway, I saw the thing about you and so I thought I'd drop into the conference and say hello. I liked the essay you wrote on creativity, too. I downloaded it from the forum library the other night.

Maybe you should write a book. <g>

Bev

> Private Mail
> Date: Thursday, July 18, 1996 11:10 a.m.
> From: Maximilian@miller&morris.com
> Subj: Good Job
> To: BevJ@frederic_gerard.com

So what do you want?

Max

> Private Mail
> Date: Thursday, July 18, 1996 1:42 p.m.
> From: BevJ@frederic_gerard.com
> Subj: Good Job
> To: Maximilian@miller&morris.com

I don't want anything, Max. I just thought it would
be nice to drop you a line and let you know I enjoyed
the conference.

But I'm sure you've already received more fan e-mail
than you have time to read from all your little
groupies.

Beverly

> Private Mail
> Date: Friday, July 19, 1996 10:36 a.m.
> From: Maximilian@miller&morris.com
> Subj: Good Job
> To: BevJ@frederic_gerard.com

Look, Bev. I don't want to fight. I'm tired of arguing
with you. It used to be fun—our going back and
forth with each other. But I don't want that anymore.

Max

> Private Mail
> Date: Friday, July 19, 1996 4:29 p.m.
> From: BevJ@frederic_gerard.com
> Subj: Good Job
> To: Maximilian@miller&morris.com

What do you want, then?

Bev

> Private Mail
> Date: Saturday, July 20, 1996 2:22 a.m.
> From: Maximilian@miller&morris.com
> Subj: Good Job
> To: BevJ@frederic_gerard.com

I want you to quit playing these games with me,

Beverly. I want you to tell me what *you* want. I want to be able to tell you what *I* want without you going off half-cocked on me, disappearing for weeks and months at a time just because I say something that makes you uncomfortable.

Maximilian

> Private Mail
> Date: Saturday, July 20, 1996 9:31 a.m.
> From: BevJ@frederic_gerard.com
> Subj: Good Job
> To: Maximilian@miller&morris.com

So tell me what you want—I won't get mad.

Bev

> Private Mail
> Date: Sunday, July 21, 1996 3:56 a.m.
> From: Maximilian@miller&morris.com
> Subj: Good Job
> To: BevJ@frederic_gerard.com

I want to talk about the night we were together. I want to relive it with you. I'm not asking you to come see me—I just want to make love to you again with my words.

> Private Mail
> Date: Friday, July 26, 1996 5:02 p.m.
> From: BevJ@frederic_gerard.com
> Subj: Good Job
> To: Maximilian@miller&morris.com

OK, Max.

GA.

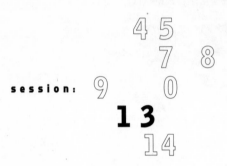

session: **13**

> Private Mail
> Date: Saturday, July 27, 1996 9:09 p.m.
> From: Maximilian@miller&morris.com
> Subj: You
> To: BevJ@frederic_gerard.com

I never had a one-night stand until that night with
you. The first time I ever had sex, believe it or not,
was the night I proposed to Tracy. Shit. I was so
clueless then. It's a good thing I called off the wed-
ding. Saved both Tracy and me from a lot of
heartache. Since then I've had a few serious relationships with women. I've also had more than a few
opportunities for one-nighters, but no matter how
trashed I might have been at the time, I never went

through with it, thank God—the thought of getting AIDS or some crap like that is always enough to sober me up at the last minute.

The first time I ever made love—I mean really made love, instead of just having sex—was with you. For some reason I felt safe going back to your room with you, even though you were a stranger to me—or so I thought at the time. The fact that you took it upon yourself to make a stop in the hotel drugstore to buy a pack of aquamarine condoms helped too. (I knew that's what you were going to do when you gave me the keys to your room and told me to meet you up there, btw. And here you thought you were being so surreptitious. ;-)

The minutes I spent waiting for you in your room were the weirdest. I'm standing in the middle of this strange hotel room, looking around at your belongings, completely aroused, completely turned on. I was so consumed with desire for you that there was no room left in my brain to question what we were doing, to think of the craziness of the situation.

I was on autopilot from the moment you smiled at me at that stupid party at the Boston Computer Museum. And yes, I noticed you had been staring at me for quite some time before then. I was enjoying the hell out of it, pretending for a while that I didn't notice you burning holes in me with your eyes. When you walked up to me and started talking I couldn't believe how calm you were, how together you seemed...how beautiful and soft you were. And there was something familiar about you—even though I knew I had never seen your face before that night, talking with you felt so comfortable, so right. There were no awkward starts and stops—the rhythm of our conversation had already been established somewhere else, at some previous point in time and space.

When we got into the taxi line together and you asked me to come back to your room with you, I wasn't surprised or shocked. I was hardly aware of what we were doing as we got into the cab together. Any other couple might have started mauling each other as soon as the cab pulled away from the curb. Not us. Our hands weren't even touching as we rested them next to each other on the back seat of the taxi. Still, I had never been so hard in my life.

Are you always that tidy when you travel? As I stood there in your room waiting for you to come back from the hotel drugstore, I could see your skirts and blouses hanging in your closet—you had them precisely arranged according to which blouse went with which skirt. Each pair of your high heels was placed just so on the closet floor. Your suitcase rested neatly on the suitcase stand next to the open closet. Your suitcase, too, was open. You had all your clothing that didn't need to be put on hangers still in the suitcase: t-shirts, jeans, socks rolled into neat little balls, and your underwear. I have never in my life met anyone who folds her underwear like that. How do you do that? And your nightshirt: an oversized white t-shirt which you had laid flat across the back of the chair; with printing on the front of it in large black letters: "Real Men Marry Editors." Where did you find something like that? Do they have merchandise catalogs with stuff made especially for all you crazy people who work in publishing?

That's what I was thinking about when you walked into the room. I heard you come in. I looked up and there you were. You stood in the middle of the room and let me look at you. No. It was more than that. You were looking at me too. I knew that you weren't thinking of this thing as letting a stranger make love to you. I knew you would make love to me, too. You didn't bother with any small talk—you took your time staring into my eyes. Then you stared at my crotch! You hussy! <g>

As aroused as I was, I didn't feel the need to hurry. The urgency, yes, but it was a slow urgency. You turned and went into the bathroom. I knew you were going to get undressed in there and that when you came out you would be naked, or at least mostly undressed. Not because of any modesty, no. I understood we would avoid the awkwardness and fumbling of trying to get undressed in front of each other or of trying to rip each other's clothes off while smashing our lips together and grabbing the backs of each other's heads, which always looks good in the movies but is anything but graceful in real life. I took your cue and slipped out of my suit, shirt, and boxers as quickly and as quietly as possible, and laid them neatly over the back of the chair—the one that didn't have your nightshirt on it, because I didn't want to mess up anything in your room.

Either I was super-efficient and got my clothes off in record time, or you took an extra-long time in the bathroom—I'm not sure which. I lifted the neatly folded covers on your bed and slipped between the sheets. I even had time to eat one of the chocolate mints that the night maid had placed on your pillow. I saved the other mint for you. (Do they always put two mints on the bed, even if they think there's supposed to be only one person staying in the room?)

When you finally opened the bathroom door and walked out into the room I felt the world stand still for a moment. You had taken off all your clothes except your underwear. What was it about your underwear? It's not as if it was exotic or even overtly sexy. I've seen a lot of women in their underwear in my time (and no—it's not what you think—I do the photo shoots for the Olivia's Boutique catalogs, remember?) but I've never seen a woman who wears her underwear quite as well as you do. It was sexier than if you had come out of the bathroom completely naked.

Where do I go from here? What words can I say to you that would even come close to evoking the things I felt the night we were together, Bev? It's Saturday night; I'm sitting here at home at my computer. With my fingers resting on the keyboard I merely have to close my eyes and rest the back of my head on the wall behind me and everything we did that night comes rushing through my mind. And through my groin. I knew I would write this message to you tonight. I cancelled my date with Steffee but

I didn't tell her why. Tonight I saved for you, for remembering you. For remembering us.

Max

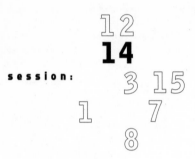

session:

> Private Mail
> Date: Sunday, July 28, 1996 10:19 a.m.
> From: BevJ@frederic_gerard.com
> Subj: You
> To: Maximilian@miller&morris.com

For a long time after that night I didn't set my watch
back to local time—I kept it set one hour ahead, for
the time zone where we were together—even though
I had been back from the trip for weeks. I didn't
know if you lived in that time zone, but it didn't
matter. I could look at my watch and know it was set
at the same time as the clocks in *our* time zone, as
the clocks in our hotel room.

I could be at work, worrying about getting to a

morning meeting on time. I'd glance at my watch, and it would say the time was 8:45 a.m. when I knew it was really only 7:45 a.m. my time. But in that brief moment looking down at my watch, I could be transported from my time zone to ours. I could be reminded that it was really 8:45 a.m. in our hotel room. And I could remember what we were doing at that exact moment in our time zone, in the only time zone that mattered.

If only I could wake up like that every morning. I thought I had let go of any of my remaining inhibitions the night before, when we spent the night making love to each other. Well, half the night. My slumber that night after we finished doing to each other everything we wanted to do, everything I wanted to do to you and everything I wanted you to do to me, was dreamless—blank and black and deep and good. Except for the dream I began to have immediately before I woke up and found you on top of me. It was a dream of being touched by no one who could know those things about me, who could know exactly the way I wanted to be touched down there—how soft, how hard, how slow, how fast, how long. I wanted the dream to go on forever but I also wanted to become conscious so I could arch myself higher, closer, to your hand. And when I opened my eyes you smiled and put yourself inside of me. You were waiting for me to come awake into your world.

The most difficult things about leaving you that morning in my hotel room as I prepared to leave for the convention was not giving you my name and phone number and making you promise you wouldn't come back that night. You asked me for my number repeatedly but I couldn't let my resolve weaken. The night we spent together was an unexpected gift and I didn't want to ruin it by getting greedy. I couldn't believe I had been allowed to have such a perfect experience at this point in my life. I was grateful then and I'm grateful now.

I knew when I left you alone in my room, lying there naked in my bed as I slipped on my heels and selected a pair of earrings to match my outfit, that you would rummage through my things, looking for something with my name on it, an address book or a plane ticket or something. So I made sure to take my Day-Timer and my plane tickets and all of that stuff in my briefcase with me to the show that day. I knew it was the right thing to do—to be thankful for what we had, to keep that night as a memory and nothing more.

I had a friend in college who would do some really crazy things, like one night during finals week he came and picked me up on his motorcycle with a picnic basket strapped onto the back of the bike, and drove me to the football field. We scaled the walls and he set out a blanket on the 50-yard line and mixed some Tanqueray-and-tonics for us and we sat there, drinking and playing charades until one of the campus rent-a-cops heard us laughing and screaming and told us to get out of there. When I asked my friend why he dreamed up adventures like that, he said, "I'm making memories."

We made a memory, Max. It was beautiful. We'll have it for the rest of our lives.

Bev

session: **15** 13 6 7 7 8 9 11

> Private Mail
> Date: Sunday, July 28, 1996 5:54 p.m.
> From: Maximilian@miller&morris.com
> Subj: Implode/Explode/Whatever
> To: BevJ@frederic_gerard.com

Bev,

I lied.

Max

> Private Mail
> Date: Monday, July 29, 1996 7:08 a.m.
> From: BevJ@frederic_gerard.com
> Subj: Implode/Explode/Whatever
> To: Maximilian@miller&morris.com

Max,

What did you lie about?

Bev

> Private Mail
> Date: Monday, July 29, 1996 9:43 a.m.
> From: Maximilian@miller&morris.com
> Subj: Implode/Explode/Whatever
> To: BevJ@frederic_gerard.com

Remember when I told you I would immediately explode if I ever saw you again?

> Private Mail
> Date: Monday, July 29, 1996 3:58 p.m.
> From: BevJ@frederic_gerard.com
> Subj: Implode/Explode/Whatever
> To: Maximilian@miller&morris.com

Yes, I remember that.

> Private Mail
> Date: Monday, July 29, 1996 6:07 p.m.
> From: Maximilian@miller&morris.com
> Subj: Implode/Explode/Whatever
> To: BevJ@frederic_gerard.com

I haven't even seen you again and I've already exploded.

That last message you sent me...

> Private Mail
> Date: Tuesday, July 30, 1996 8:17 a.m.
> From: BevJ@frederic_gerard.com
> Subj: Implode/Explode/Whatever
> To: Maximilian@miller&morris.com

Look who's talking! That message you sent *me*...

Bev

> Private Mail
> Date: Tuesday, July 30, 1996 11:33 a.m.
> From: Maximilian@miller&morris.com
> Subj: Implode/Explode/Whatever
> To: BevJ@frederic_gerard.com

If we keep this up, I'm going to be forced into buying that new computer I keep talking about.

> Private Mail
> Date: Tuesday, July 30, 1996 2:10 p.m.
> From: BevJ@frederic_gerard.com
> Subj: Implode/Explode/Whatever
> To: Maximilian@miller&morris.com

And why is that?

> Private Mail
> Date: Tuesday, July 30, 1996 4:49 p.m.
> From: Maximilian@miller&morris.com
> Subj: Implode/Explode/Whatever
> To: BevJ@frederic_gerard.com

Well, you know...my keyboard is starting to get sticky.

> Private Mail
> Date: Tuesday, July 30, 1996 7:28 p.m.
> From: BevJ@frederic_gerard.com
> Subj: Implode/Explode/Whatever
> To: Maximilian@miller&morris.com

Oh, Max! That's gross! I don't want to know about it!

> Private Mail
> Date: Wednesday, July 31, 1996 9:01 a.m.
> From: Maximilian@miller&morris.com
> Subj: Implode/Explode/Whatever
> To: BevJ@frederic_gerard.com

I'm just trying to warn you so you won't be surprised when I send you the bill for my new computer. ;-)

> Private Mail
> Date: Wednesday, July 31, 1996 12:10 p.m.
> From: BevJ@frederic_gerard.com
> Subj: Implode/Explode/Whatever
> To: Maximilian@miller&morris.com

Oh, I see. So that's how it works? Well then. In that case I think it's paramount that you buy absolutely the cheapest computer you can find. That's my advice and I'm sticking to it (pun intended).

;-)

Bev

> Private Mail
> Date: Wednesday, July 31, 1996 2:21 p.m.
> From: Maximilian@miller&morris.com
> Subj: Sticky Business
> To: BevJ@frederic_gerard.com

Bev,

I really think it would be helpful to me if you would just come here and help me shop for the computer in person.

Max

> Private Mail
> Date: Thursday, August 1, 1996 5:14 a.m.
> From: BevJ@frederic_gerard.com
> Subj: Sticky Business
> To: Maximilian@miller&morris.com

Max,

What are you doing tomorrow night?

Bev

> Private Mail
> Date: Thursday, August 1, 1996 8:28 a.m.
> From: Maximilian@miller&morris.com
> Subj: Sticky Business
> To: BevJ@frederic_gerard.com

You mean you're going to come see me?

> Private Mail
> Date: Thursday, August 1, 1996 9:42 a.m.
> From: BevJ@frederic_gerard.com
> Subj: Sticky Business
> To: Maximilian@miller&morris.com

No, I was thinking we could meet each other in one of the forum conference rooms for a live chat.

> Private Mail
> Date: Thursday, August 1, 1996 11:16 a.m.
> From: Maximilian@miller&morris.com
> Subj: Sticky Business
> To: BevJ@frederic_gerard.com

Like last October—when I told you who I was and you stormed off and wouldn't speak to me again for months?

> Private Mail
> Date: Thursday, August 1, 1996 2:11 p.m.
> From: BevJ@frederic_gerard.com
> Subj: Sticky Business
> To: Maximilian@miller&morris.com

Well, no. I was hoping we wouldn't get into a humongoid fight this time.

> Private Mail
> Date: Thursday, August 1, 1996 3:49 p.m.
> From: Maximilian@miller&morris.com
> Subj: Sticky Business
> To: BevJ@frederic_gerard.com

I'll try my best not to piss you off, Bev. What time do you want to meet?

> Private Mail
> Date: Friday, August 2, 1996 8:21 a.m.
> From: BevJ@frederic_gerard.com
> Subj: Sticky Business
> To: Maximilian@miller&morris.com

Just as long as you don't spring any surprises on me this time, Max.

Would 9:00 p.m. "our time" work well for you? Same place as before?

> Private Mail
> Date: Friday, August 2, 1996 10:16 a.m.
> From: Maximilian@miller&morris.com
> Subj: Sticky Business
> To: BevJ@frederic_gerard.com

That would be perfect. See you then.

> Friday, August 2, 1996   9:19 p.m.

> Writer's Forum   > Live Chat   > People Here: 2

(Private)

| Maximilian: | You're late. :-(|
| BevJ: | Sorry! I was worried you wouldn't still be here. I ended up having to work late. Then there was a traffic jam on my way home, so it took forever to get out of the city. And then when I finally got home and walked into my office, my cat had coughed up a bunch of hairballs and gunk like that all over |

	the carpet. I wanted to get it cleaned up before I logged on so I wouldn't have to smell cat puke while I was talking with you.
Maximilian:	You're so romantic, Bev.
BevJ:	I'm just glad you were still here when I finally logged on, Max. Thanks for waiting for me.
Maximilian:	No problem. I was sitting here reading Dave Barry's new book, Dave Barry in Cyberspace, while I waited for you.
Bevj:	Really? Is it a good book? I love Dave Barry.
Maximilian:	It's hilarious. He's got this section in the book where he lists all the different emoticons and explains what they mean, including a bunch of symbols he obviously made up, like one for a person giving birth to a squirrel.
BevJ:	LOL. I'll have to look for that next time I'm in the bookstore.
Maximilian:	But you didn't ask me here tonight to talk about books, did you?
BevJ:	Not exactly. But that's OK. :-)
Maximilian:	So what did you want to talk about?
BevJ:	Nothing in particular, really. I just thought it would be a nice change of pace for us to have a live chat—a conversation in which we didn't have time to ponder our responses to each other, where we could be a little more spontaneous.
Maximilian:	You're getting into this spontaneity

	thing, aren't you, Bev?
	When I first met you online, you were sort of a, how shall I say . . . control freak.
BevJ:	Yeah, I know. I'm trying to be better about that, Max.
Maximilian:	And you're doing a damn fine job, Bev. So. What's your bra size?
BevJ:	Ha ha.
Maximilian:	Isn't that, like, a cyberspace pickup line?
BevJ:	Yes, but not a very successful one, in my experience.
Maximilian:	OK then. How about this one: Excuse me, ma'am, but could you give me advice on which computer I should buy? <weg>
BevJ:	*Now* you're getting me excited! <g>
Max:	}:-)
BevJ:	So where's Steffee tonight?
Maximilian:	At her apartment. I told her I was going to stay in tonight and do some work on my computer. Which isn't exactly a lie. Where's Gary?
BevJ:	Working late. He's rushing to finish a big project. So . . . you and Steffee are still going together, huh?
Maximilian:	You make it sound as if we're in junior high and I've given her my ID bracelet, Bev.
BevJ:	Sorry. Didn't mean to... Are you guys sleeping together?
Maximilian:	What kind of question is that?

BevJ:	I guess you could say it was a fairly direct question. :-*
Maximilian:	Oh, now you're sending me kisses through cyberspace. That's a first. :-* backatcha.
BevJ:	You're avoiding my question.
Maximilian:	Not particularly. I was just savoring my first cyberkiss. :-)

Maximilian:	Bev? Are you still there?
BevJ:	Yes. I was waiting for you to answer my question.
Maximilian:	I feel like this is a setup.
BevJ:	How so?
Maximilian:	Like you'll use my answer as an excuse to get mad at me, to vanish again into the ether and never come back. I don't want to lose you again, Bev.
BevJ:	I promise I won't vanish like I did before. But from what you just said I can pretty much figure out that you *are* sleeping with her.
Maximilian:	Yes, I am. Come on, Bev. This is the '90s, remember? I've been seeing her for six months now.
BevJ:	I know... <sigh>
Maximilian:	Bev, I was wondering—how do you know these conversations we're having are completely private? Couldn't someone be listening to—or watching—what we're saying to each other right now?

BevJ:	Max, it's not as if we're in a public chat room, where everyone can see everyone else's responses. This is a private room. And if someone else were here, listening to our conversation, the system would let us know that someone new had entered the room, and the "People Here" number in the top right corner of your screen would change from 2 to 3.
	But I can't promise you unequivocally that absolutely no one can read our messages to each other, even when they're supposed to be private.
Maximilian:	You mean all that stuff you hear about hackers in cyberspace is true?
BevJ:	Well, I don't know about all of it, but I'm sure a lot of it is for real.
Maximilian:	I guess we should try to be more careful, then.
BevJ:	Max, we've already thrown caution to the wind. If someone's been reading our messages up to now, then we'd have to do some serious backpedaling to disentangle ourselves from this one.
Maximilian:	Oh. In that case...what *is* your bra size?
BevJ:	Come on, Max. You can do better than that! :-)
BevJ:	Max?
Maximilian:	Bev?

BevJ:	Did you realize Macworld is coming up again in Boston next weekend?
Maximilian:	Yes, I was aware of that. Are you going?
BevJ:	Yes. Are you?
Maximilian:	I wasn't planning to. Would you meet me there if I did go?
BevJ:	Like, what—for dinner or something?
Maximilian:	We could do dinner, sure. But I was thinking more about the "or something" part.
BevJ:	This would be an awfully big step for us, Max. We could be making a huge mistake.
Maximilian:	True. It could also be the best thing that ever happened to us—even better than before. You know what I've been fantasizing about ever since we connected again, Bev?
BevJ:	No—what?
Maximilian:	About being able to make love with you again, like we did that night, only this time, I could whisper your name into your ear while I'm inside of you.
BevJ:	Would you bring the talking condom?
Maximilian:	Of course. <g>
BevJ:	Is there still time for you to get a plane ticket?
Maximilian:	I don't have to get a flight. I can drive up from New York.
BevJ:	So that's where you are.

Maximilian:	It doesn't take a brain surgeon to fig-ure out that I'm in New York, Bev—after all, you knew I worked for an ad agency.
BevJ:	It's not as if there aren't ad agencies in other cities, Max. God! I hope you're not one of those people who thinks New York is the center of the universe.
Maximilian:	You're the center of my universe, Bev.
BevJ:	I'm staying at the same hotel I stayed at last year, Max.
Maximilian:	I can meet you there Friday night in time for dinner.
BevJ:	I'll pencil you in. ;-)
Maximilian:	Bev, I'm going to log off now—quit while I'm ahead and all that. :-) I can't wait to see you again.
BevJ:	OK, I'll log off too for now.
BevJ:	Max?
%System%:	Maximilian has left the forum.
BevJ:	I love you.

online glossary

acronyms & abbreviations

AFK	away from keyboard
AOL	America Online
BG	big grin
BPS	bits per second
BTW	by the way
CIS	CompuServe Information Service
CO	conference
CUL	see you later
CULA	see you later alligator
F2F	face-to-face
FWIW	for what it's worth
FYI	for your information
G	grin
G,D&R	grinning, ducking & running
G,D&RVVF	grinning, ducking & running very very fast
GA	go ahead
GMTA	great minds think alike

HTML	HyperText Markup Language
IMA	I might add
IMHO	in my humble opinion
IMNSHO	in my not-so-humble opinion
IMO	in my opinion
LOL	laughing out loud
Net	short for Internet
OTOH	on the other hand
PMFJI	pardon me for jumping in
ROFLOL	rolling on floor laughing out loud
RSN	real soon now
TIA	thanks in advance
TPTB	the powers that be
VBG	very big grin
Web	short for World Wide Web
WEG	wicked evil grin
WWW	World Wide Web

emoticons & other symbols

:-)	smile
;-)	wink
:-(	frown
:-*	kiss
:'-(	crying
}:-)	horny smile
< > or :: ::	signifies something that the writer is doing or pretending to do, such as <sigh> or ::going to get body oil now::
>>>>	indicates that the words following this symbol are being quoted from another message
* * or _ _	indicates emphasis of the word or phrase typed inside these symbols

colophon

The typefaces used in this book are Faktos and Bell
Gothic Black for the chapter heads and Adobe
Caslon and Adobe Caslon Expert for the body text.

ABOUT THE AUTHOR

NAN MCCARTHY WAS BORN IN CHICAGO IN 1961 AND IS A FORMER COMPUTER JOURNALIST. CHAT, CONNECT, AND CRASH ARE NAN'S FIRST NOVELS. SHE IS CURRENTLY WORKING ON HER NEXT BOOK, A BLUES NOVEL SET IN THE SOUTH SIDE OF CHICAGO. NAN LIVES IN GRAYSLAKE, ILLINOIS WITH HER HUSBAND, THEIR TWO SONS, ONE DOG, FIVE CATS, AND AN AMAZING GOLDFISH NAMED ELVIS. YOU CAN VISIT NAN'S WEB SITE AT HTTP://WWW.RAINWATER.COM OR WRITE TO HER AT NAN@RAINWATER.COM